USBORNE

QUEST of the GODS

"AN ANCIENT EGYPTIAN PROPHECY AND A CHALLENGING QUEST TO FREE THE GODS – IF YOU LIKE AN EPIC ADVENTURE STORY COMBINED WITH GREAT ILLUSTRATIONS, YOU'LL LOVE THIS."

DR JULIE ANDERSON,
DEPARTMENT OF ANCIENT EGYPT AND SUDAN
THE BRITISH MUSEUM

With thanks to Adrian Bott

First published in the UK in 2013 by Usborne Publishing Ltd.,
Usborne House, 83-85 Saffron Hill, London EC1N 8RT, England.
www.usborne.com

Cover illustration by Staz Johnson. Inside illustrations by David Shephard.
Map by Ian McNee.

With thanks to Anne Millard for historical consultancy.

A CIP catalogue record for this book is available from the British Library.

ISBN 9781409562016 JFM MJJASOND/13 02926/1
Printed in Dongguan, Guangdong, China.

INTO THE UNDERWORLD

Fight of the Falcon God

DAN HUNTER

The Sacred Coffin Text of Pharaoh Akori

I shall sail rightly in my vessel
I am Lord of Eternity
in the crossing of the sky.

Let my heart speak truth;
Let me not suffer
the torments of the wicked!

For the Great Devourer awaits,
And the forty-two demons
howl around the Hall of Judgement.

Let me hold my head upright in honour,
and be spared the claws and teeth
of the Shrieking Ones.

The Eaters of Bones,
let them not touch me.
The Drinkers of Blood,
let them not come near me.
The Winged Ones with Jaws of Iron,
may they pass me by.

And may I remain safe
in the presence of Osiris forever.

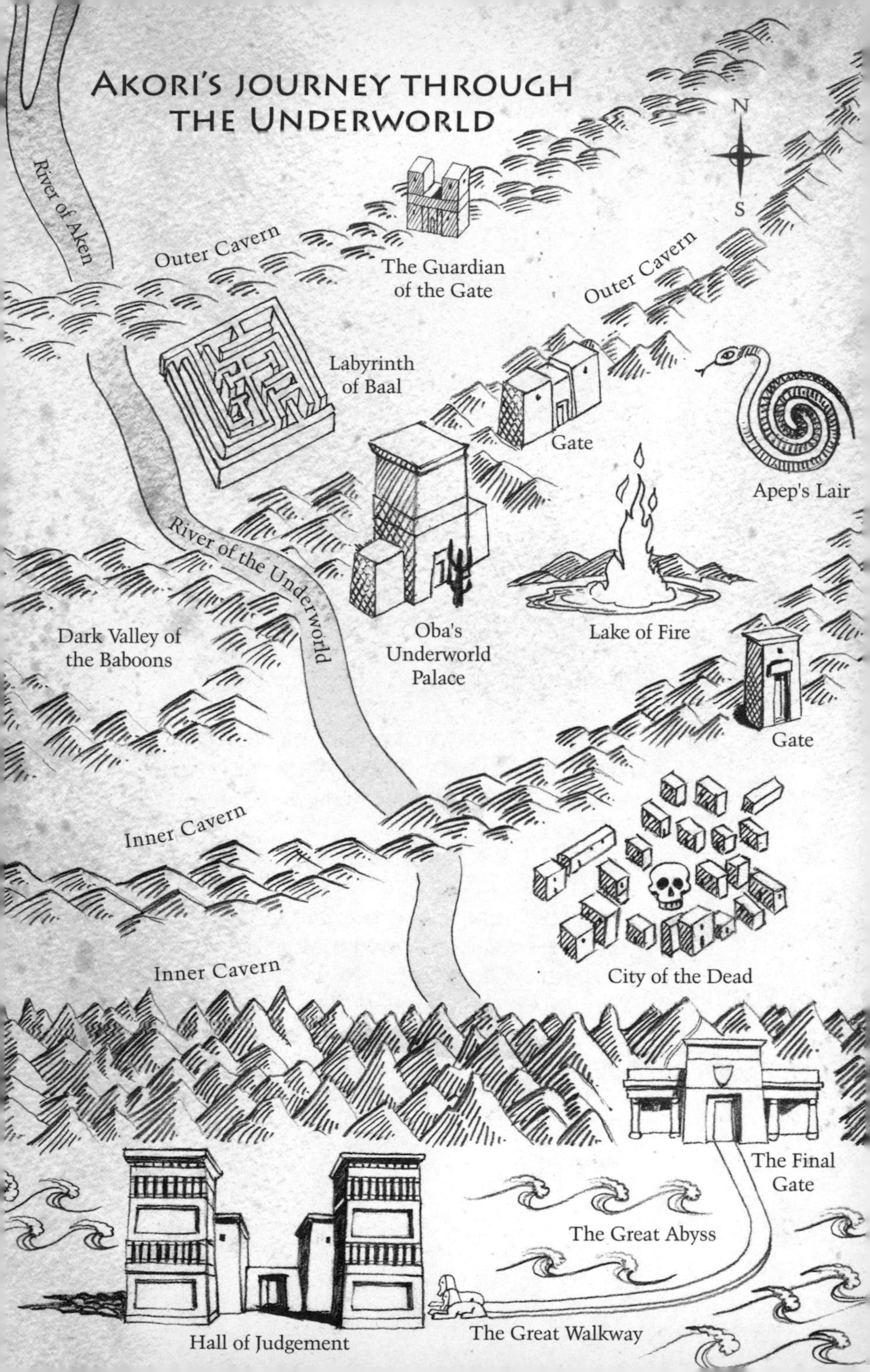

Akori's Journey Through
the Underworld
N
S
River of Aken
Outer Cavern
The Guardian
of the Gate
Outer Cavern
Labyrinth
of Baal
Gate
Apep's Lair
River of the Underworld
Dark Valley of
the Baboons
Oba's
Underworld
Palace
Lake of Fire
Gate
Inner Cavern
Inner Cavern
City of the Dead
The Final
Gate
The Great Abyss
Hall of Judgement
The Great Walkway

Prologue

The boy stood on the shores of a lake of fire and stared down into the never-ending flames. Back when he had been Pharaoh in the world of the living, he had enjoyed looking into the fire. Back then, it made him think of destruction, suffering and other things he loved. Now he thought only of revenge.

The boy's name was Oba, and he was alive. This was not, in itself, a remarkable thing; but here, in the realm where the dead came to be judged, to be living *was strange and terrible. The souls of the dead stared at him. Their jaws gaped. The monstrous creatures that dwelled in this cavern of the Underworld glared at him with hatred and licked their lips. It would have driven grown men insane with fear, let alone normal boys. But Oba wasn't afraid, neither of the dead nor of the monsters. He was under the protection of a being far more fearsome than they could ever be.*

An ugly wound lay like a badly ploughed furrow across the smooth skin of Oba's chest. He fingered it now and thought back over how close he had come to death. Images flashed through his mind. The golden blade plunged into his chest in that final fight. The sweating face of the boy who had shoved it there. Oba's protector had saved his life, but the magic had hurt. Oba grimaced. He remembered the fingertip that had seared like a red-hot poker, the blistering pain. The wound had burned. The blood had scalded his skin like droplets of hot oil. Oba had screamed, wept and screamed again for nine days and nights, but he had lived.

That had been when he was new to the Underworld. Set's dark blessing had passed into his flesh since then. Fire hardly bothered him at all now.

"Akori," he said, spitting out the name as he had done so many times. "Farm boy oaf. You did this. You defeated my allies with your filthy tricks. You dared to shed my royal blood!" His voice was like a reptile's hiss. "Powers of the Underworld!" Oba called out across the flames. "Show me what Akori is doing now!"

Obediently, the flames coiled and twined into an image. Oba peered eagerly at it as it took form. He prayed to all the dark Gods that he would see Akori suffering. Perhaps Akori was sick, dying slowly and painfully. Perhaps he had been thrown from a horse and broken a bone. Better still, perhaps a cobra had bitten him, and he was writhing in agony at this very moment, soon to make the journey to the Underworld himself…

But the boy whose face finally appeared in the flames did not seem to be dying. He wasn't even in pain. He was laughing.

"No!" Oba wailed.

Akori was leaning back in the Pharaoh's throne in the main room of the royal palace, laughing and cracking jokes with someone Oba couldn't see. The Double Crown of Egypt was on his head, proclaiming him the ruler of both the Upper and Lower Kingdoms.

"That throne doesn't belong to you!" Oba screamed. "It's mine! It's all *mine! Give it back!* Give it baaaack!*"*

Akori couldn't hear Oba's furious screams. He went on smiling and talking as if everything was just fine.

Oba couldn't bear it. He sank to his knees,

beat the sand with his fists and let out a howl of cheated rage.

A huge black fist thrust through the image of Akori. It abruptly broke apart into fiery shards.

Oba started. His eyes widened. "My Lord?" he whispered, suddenly quiet. "Is that you?"

Set, the Lord of Storms, strode up from the lake of fire. He brushed a burning ember from his broad chest as if it were a stray wisp of cotton. Tall as a giant, with the head of some strange beast, like a cross between an ass and a pig, he was Oba's protector and ally.

"You seem distressed, my young friend," Set said to him. Everything about the God was filth, fire and darkness. Even his voice was like molten tar bubbling in a cauldron.

"It's Akori," Oba said hoarsely. "You saw him! Living in my palace, smirking like the

idiot he is. He thinks he's so clever. He thinks he's won. I want to wipe that smile off his stupid face."

"In that case," Set gloated, "I have some good news for you."

Oba's eyes bulged with astonishment. "Good news? You mean – the plan? It's finally ready?"

"Indeed!" Set laughed. "I struck like thunder from the darkness, and defeated Osiris before he knew I was upon him!"

A horrible grin spread across Oba's face. He couldn't believe Osiris, God of the Underworld, had been beaten by Set.

"Osiris now lies imprisoned," Set said. He laid a smouldering hand upon Oba's shoulder. "It is time you and I began to make plans for our conquest."

Oba's flesh sizzled under Set's touch, but he didn't care. He was grinning like a maniac; revenge was within his grasp at last. Let Akori smile while he still could. Soon, the armies of the dead would haul him down from his stolen throne, pull the crown from his head, cut the head from his body and send his soul screaming into the Underworld.

Yes, Oba would have the last laugh, after all. And what a long, cruel laugh it would be.

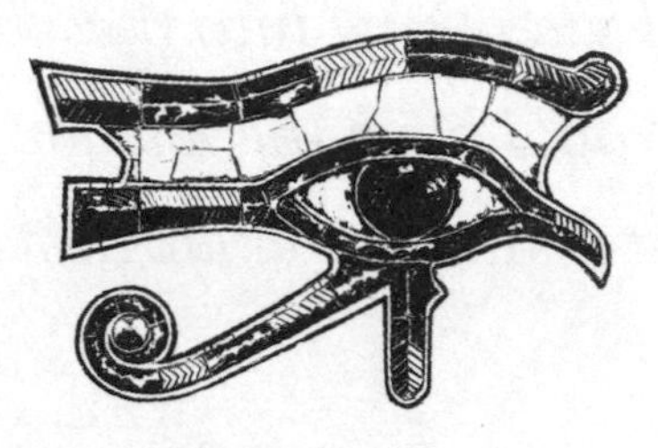

CHAPTER ONE

The Pharaoh Akori sat beside his new High Priest of Horus, Manu. His brow was furrowed in concentration.

"Come on, My Pharaoh," laughed Manu. "Time's running out! You're not going to let me beat you at a riddle contest, are you?"

When Oba had reigned, the royal palace had been a darkened, shadowy place of fear and hushed whispers. Now the daylight shone on carved columns and colourful wall paintings, ornamental chairs of gilded wood, and hangings of fine white linen. A few cats lounged in the sunny spots, because cats in this kingdom came and went as they pleased, even in the courts of kings.

All around, the gathered palace staff looked on expectantly. Nobody said a word, but everyone was smiling, from the officials with their scrolls and shaven heads to the guards at the doors, even down to the servants who kneeled with their trays of food and pitchers of water. When Oba had been on the throne, they would have been silent out of fear. Not any more.

"I should have challenged you to a wrestling match, Manu!" Akori joked. "But you're so skinny, you'd snap like a dry twig!"

Manu rested his chin on his fist. "You could always give up," he teased. "Let your High Priest win for a change. Wouldn't that be refreshing?"

"Never!"

"Very well. I'll repeat the riddle one last time. The man who makes it doesn't want it for himself, but the man who uses it will have it for ever. What is it?"

Akori racked his brains, trying to think of what the answer could be. Once, he might have been angry at his friend Manu for pitching such a brain-teaser – was the priest trying to make him look stupid in front of his court? But he knew Manu was really showing him great respect. Akori was Pharaoh now, and a Pharaoh needed to be a thinker as well as a fighter. Manu wasn't going to make it easy for him, not even by letting him win a simple riddle contest.

What sort of thing would a man use for ever? Most objects got used up or thrown away over the course of your life. Even a house would be useless after you were dead.

But wait – maybe that was what the riddle meant! Something that was yours for ever after you died...

"A coffin!" Akori shouted triumphantly. "That's the answer!"

Manu bowed his head, graciously accepting his defeat.

Victory! The officials clapped politely, the guards yelled and cheered and banged their spear hafts on the floor, and the servants made whooping noises and danced on the spot.

Akori stood up smiling, and called for quiet. "Once again, your Pharaoh has beaten his loyal High Priest at a game of skill. I declare this lunch break over! Chancellor Imhotep, what's this afternoon's business?"

A small, fat official came forward, scroll in hand. "Ambassadors to receive from Athens, My Pharaoh, and harvest reports from the southern kingdoms to look over—" He stopped and frowned.

The light in the room, already bright, was becoming blinding. Murmurs broke out. From somewhere in the distance came the sound of rushing winds, roaring over the rooftops, howling around the palace. The hangings blew inwards and flew like flags in a gale.

Akori felt cold excitement in the pit of his stomach. His arm was tingling. That only ever meant one thing! He glanced down. Sure enough, his falcon-shaped birthmark was glowing fiercely.

Manu looked at it, looked at him, and they both grinned. "Horus!" they said together.

Akori swept his arms outwards as if he were parting the sea. "Everyone, stand back!"

The crowds hurried away from the centre of the room. A column of dazzling golden light slammed down into the space. People gasped. In the column's midst a huge figure appeared. He had the head of a falcon and the body of a powerful warrior.

Everyone in the room fell to one knee in worship. The God Horus was here, come to visit his champion, the Pharaoh Akori.

Akori himself was shaking with excitement. Horus had not appeared to him since that fateful day when the future of all Egypt had hung in the balance. Then, still a farm boy, Akori had faced the almost impossible challenge of freeing five of the good Gods, including Horus himself, from Set's magical prisons. When this was complete, Akori had become Pharaoh and his life had changed for ever. But why was Horus here now?

"Akori," said Horus. His mighty voice echoed around the room like a roll of thunder, shaking the shutters and toppling a vase from its stand. "I must speak with you urgently. I have need of my champion once more!"

Horus wasn't just troubled by whatever new evil had arisen. He sounded grief-stricken. The God of Light had sounded that way only once before, when his own mother, the Goddess Isis, had been imprisoned by Set. But that couldn't have happened again... could it?

The crowds of onlookers began to mutter anxiously among themselves. If Akori didn't do something, rumours would get out of control.

"Everyone, please leave the room!" Akori commanded. "Except you, Manu. I need you with me."

"Yes, My Pharaoh." Their earlier jokes were instantly forgotten.

Horus did not speak again until only Akori and Manu were left facing him.

"My father, Osiris, God of the Dead, is the rightful Lord of the Underworld," Horus began. "But Set has turned against him. He persuaded a group of Gods to rebel and join his evil cause, and together they have imprisoned Osiris!"

Akori struggled to take the news in. He could hardly believe that five minutes ago, he and Manu had been laughing together. Everything had seemed so secure, with the kingdom safe, the people happy...but now his old foe, Set, was working his evil once again.

"Set has a champion, too," Horus said bitterly. "You know his name already."

"Oba!" Akori could hardly have forgotten the evil, mocking boy who had usurped the Pharaoh's throne. "I should have killed him when I had the chance," he groaned.

"You very nearly did," Horus said. "You struck a killing blow. Set saved Oba's life with dark magic. Oba is no longer a mortal boy. He is part demon."

"Lord Horus," said Manu, who had turned very pale. "I do not understand. Your father Osiris is the judge of the dead – but if he has been imprisoned, then who is judging the dead now?"

"Nobody," said Horus darkly.

"But without their judge, how can the dead pass on to the afterlife?"

"They cannot. The dead are remaining in the outer caverns of the Underworld. Their numbers are increasing. Anubis, the good God who guides the dead, believes Oba and Set are plotting to gather them into a huge army. Once the army is complete, they will unleash it upon Egypt. Oba will reclaim his throne and rule over a nation of enslaved Egyptians, backed by the power of Set."

"So that's their plan," Akori said. "My Lord, we have to stop them. I'm ready. Tell me what I must do."

"Me too!" said Manu quickly. "Don't even think of forbidding me to come, Akori. We've been through too much together. High Priest or not, I'm with you."

Akori grabbed Manu's offered hand in a brotherly grip.

"I warn you," Horus told them, "there are dangers ahead like nothing you have faced before. Osiris has been imprisoned in a dungeon beneath his Hall of Judgement, right at the very heart of the Underworld. To get to him, you will have to follow the perilous path taken by the dead."

Akori heard Manu swallow hard. He couldn't blame him. The priest knew better than Akori what horrors awaited the dead in their journey through the Underworld.

An old, cold fear was creeping into his bones. He had faced down evil Gods, battled monsters, and won a kingdom...but to enter the Underworld itself, and follow in the footsteps of the dead? No living person had ever done that before – except one; evil Oba, who was no longer fully human.

He took a deep breath and summoned up his courage. "I'll do it," he said.

"I knew I could rely upon your bravery," Horus said. "And I have not come to you empty-handed. This will help to protect you." He held out something that looked like a short-sleeved tunic made of overlapping golden scales. A small breastplate along the collar held five hollow sockets in a curved pattern. They looked as if jewels or stones had been prised out of them.

Akori took it, and placed it over his head, amazed at how light it was. "It's armour!"

"The armour of Montu, God of Battle," Horus replied. "For you have many battles to fight, Akori, if you are to free my father from Set and Oba. Five Gods will stand in your path, each of them a part of a spell that Set has woven. Your first task is to open the Gate to the deeper Underworld."

"One of those Gods must be Set himself," Akori said gravely. "But who are the others?"

"I'm afraid I do not know what horrors await you," Horus said apologetically. "You will only learn who your opponents are as you make your journey. But you must defeat them and reclaim the Pharaoh Stones if you are to have any hope of defeating Set."

"Stones? What stones?"

Manu answered before Horus could speak. "They are ancient sources of magic forged by

Ptah himself, the builder of the Universe! Osiris was appointed as the guardian of the Stones, until a Pharaoh arose who was worthy to bear them. That has never happened. Each Stone is said to represent one of the qualities of the ideal Pharaoh: strength, speed, courage, intelligence and honour."

"When Set defeated my father, Osiris, he stole the sacred Pharaoh Stones and gave them to his monstrous servants, filling them with power," Horus explained. "You must reclaim the Stones and place them in the armour. Then their power will transfer to you. Once you have all five, you will have a chance of overcoming Set and Oba."

A question was gnawing at Akori's mind – a question he didn't really want to ask. "Last time I faced Set, you were there too. But you can't help me this time, can you?"

"No," Horus said. "By entering the Underworld as a living soul, you are placing yourself beyond our help. Only those who travel with you can help you."

Akori looked down at his new golden armour. He still had his *khopesh* sword, the gift of Horus from the last quest. He'd just have to hope they would see him through the battles to come. And he'd have Manu's advice, which had saved his life in the past. But if his last quest had seemed hard, this new one seemed all but impossible.

"I must give you one last warning," Horus said. "After each battle, you must make it back out of the Underworld by sunrise. If you do not, then the Underworld will claim you for ever. Your mortal body will perish, and your soul will join the ranks of the dead."

Akori was grateful to have been given the armour of Montu, God of Battle, for his next quest. It fitted him like a well-tailored tunic, as if it had been meant for him alone. The light shining from Horus's body made patterns of dancing lights on the walls and floor where it reflected off the armour.

"How do we get to the Underworld?" Akori asked.

"Go to the valley across the Nile where the Pharaohs of old are entombed at the Necropolis of Waset," Horus told him. "Seek for one tomb among many."

"Which one?"

"The one that bears your name, and waits to receive you!"

His *own* tomb? An awful feeling came over Akori, as if scarabs were crawling under his skin.

"Open the door to your own burial chamber. Inside is a coffin, ready to take you to the Underworld. This bears a spell which you must recite. You must be there by sunset, or the spell will fail and our only chance will be lost."

"What about my kingdom?" Akori demanded, duty overcoming fear. "I'm Pharaoh now. I can't just walk away from my people! Someone will have to take care of Egypt while I'm gonc."

"You will find just the person for the job waiting outside," Horus said, and for the first time since he had appeared he sounded amused. "I must leave you now. Good luck, my champion. May your journey be swift and safe."

And with that, Horus vanished.

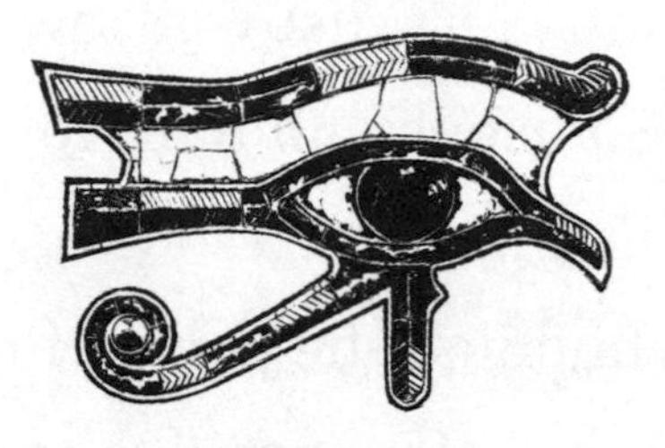

CHAPTER TWO

Akori rushed to the door and flung it open.

"Hello, old friend," smiled the wizened man who stood waiting for him. His eyes were blank, white and unseeing, but he knew Akori was there.

Akori embraced him, delighted beyond words to see him again. Horus had been right. Who better to trust with running the kingdom than the old High Priest of Horus? Together, Akori and Manu gently led the old

High Priest to a seat, and sat down on either side of him.

"I'm so happy to see you again," Akori said. "It's been *months*."

"Surprised to see me too, by the sound of it," the High Priest scoffed. "Thought I was ready for my tomb, did you? Well, I may be old, but they haven't embalmed me yet, Ra be praised!" Then he smiled and patted Akori's shoulder. "It is good to be here, Akori...My Pharaoh. And Manu, my worthy successor. I'm proud to help you. I just wish it could have been under happier circumstances."

"We all do," said Manu with a shudder. "Osiris imprisoned, Set preparing an army of the dead... I can hardly believe it."

"We should leave as soon as possible," said Akori.

"Yes you should. But eat first," said the old

High Priest. "It might be the last chance you get for a long time."

As Pharaoh, Akori could call for a feast whenever he wanted. It only took moments for the servants to prepare tables laden with freshly-baked bread, olives, roast meats, grilled fish, heaps of grapes and figs.

"Praise the Gods for the bounty of the earth," the High Priest said, making a blessing sign.

They all sat down. Akori reached straight for a roasted goose leg.

"The Gods *have* been good to Egypt," he said gratefully. "Now, everyone's going to bed with full bellies. The grain stores are all overflowing, and the fish are practically jumping into the nets."

"Akori's made sure to honour the Gods on their feast days," Manu said, as if he wanted to reassure the old High Priest that he'd been doing his job properly.

"They also tell me," the High Priest said knowingly, "that the Pharaoh has taken better care of his kingdom's farmers than any other Pharaoh in history. The Gods may make the seeds grow, Manu, but human workers sowed those seeds. Remember them, too, when you are thanking the Gods."

Manu turned as red as a boiled beetroot. "Of course," he stammered.

To spare his old friend's feelings, Akori changed the subject. "Ebe would love a piece of that fish, wouldn't she? I wish she was here."

Manu nodded. "Me too. I know it's been months since she left us, but I still keep turning around and expecting to see her there."

"Because she always *was* there, when we needed her," Akori said.

"I miss her too," the old High Priest said mournfully. "To think I always thought she was just a mute slave girl! And yet she was a Goddess all along – the Cat Goddess Bast in human form, accompanying you on your quest."

"She saved my life so many times," Akori sighed. "Remember, Manu?"

Manu began to count on his fingers. "That time you went to free Ra from the Snake Goddess Wadjet, Ebe turned into her giant cat form and fought her off. She fought hundreds of those mummies when we were trying to free Anubis. She almost got herself killed when we were freeing Isis from Sobek, the Crocodile God, and that horrible Frog Goddess wife of his. We wouldn't have made it to Sekhmet's prison without her help. She even chased off Anat and Astarte, Set's demonic wives. And then—"

"Then we had the hardest fight of all, against a whole army!" Akori cut in. "Outside this very palace!"

"Ebe turned into her giant cat form before our eyes."

"I couldn't believe what I was seeing!"

"I can't believe she isn't coming with us this time," Manu said gloomily. "Akori, I know Horus would never ask you to do the impossible, but..."

"I know," Akori said with a warning glance. He'd had the same thought. How could they hope to succeed with so little help?

On their last quest, in which he'd had to free five of the great Gods of Egypt, Ebe had been with them the whole way, a disguised Goddess helping them secretly. Now she was gone, back among her fellow Gods. Not only that, but the gifts that the Gods had given

Akori were gone, too. He would have to enter the Underworld without them. He wished he still had the Scarab of Anubis that could heal almost any wound, or the Ring of Isis to make himself invisible.

But the Gods had needed to take their treasures back. Magic objects that were forged in the realm of the Gods could not stay in the world of men for long, or they would lose their power completely.

At least I still have my sword, Akori thought. The golden *khopesh*, shaped like a large sickle, was his by right. Unlike the other treasures of the Gods, this one belonged to him alone; it was the sign he was Horus's chosen champion. That enchanted sword had slashed through solid iron as easily as hacking down a reed.

"Well, one thing's for certain," Manu said, picking at his food. "We can't tell the people of Egypt that their Pharaoh is off to the Underworld to battle the dark Gods. They'd panic."

"We need a cover story," Akori said. "We could tell them I'm ill."

"Nobody would believe that," Manu scoffed. "You did your ceremonial run at the coronation, to prove your fitness!"

Manu was right. Tradition demanded that the Pharaoh perform a run around his entire lands, to show he was fit enough to rule the kingdom.

"Perhaps an official trip?" the old High Priest suggested. "Akori could be visiting relatives in the far south."

"I don't have any relatives," protested Akori. "Uncle Shenti was the only family I ever knew and he's dead."

"But you *are* from a distant branch of the royal family. Maybe Manu could find an old scroll somewhere in the archives, showing relatives you never knew you had?"

"I'm sure I can fake – sorry, I mean *find* – something like that," said Manu with a wink.

Akori nodded. "Good. It's settled, then. Let's quickly gather our provisions and leave right away."

The news spread quickly through the palace. The Pharaoh was leaving, taking only Manu, the High Priest with him. Some sort of journey to visit royal relatives, blessed by Horus himself.

Alone in his royal chamber, Akori rummaged through his racks of clothes. Then he found what he was looking for and held it up triumphantly. A plain, dark cloak. He put it on. It completely covered up the gleaming coat of armour Horus had given him. Akori looked at himself in a polished metal mirror. "Now I look just like any other Egyptian," he said to himself. "Good. The last thing I want is someone recognizing me on the way. Especially when I'm supposed to be at the other end of the country."

Filled with fresh confidence, he grabbed his *khopesh* and slipped out through a back door, making his way quickly through the corridors. Only the moon-eyed palace cats watched his departure; and, as is the way of cats, they said nothing about it to anyone.

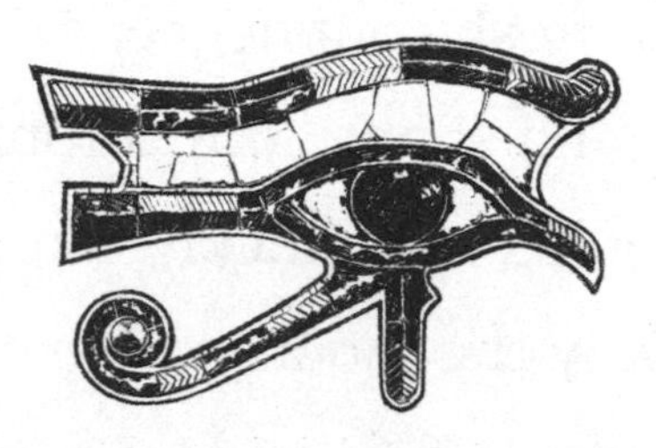

CHAPTER THREE

The palace's rear doors were so rarely used, Akori had expected to find the passage dark and deserted. When he saw a single oil lamp burning beside the arch, he narrowed his eyes and reached for his sword. Two figures were waiting, their shadows huge on the hieroglyph-covered wall. He rubbed his eyes and looked again. He breathed out in relief. It was only Manu and the High Priest, here to meet him for the departure.

"You shouldn't have lit the lamp!" he said,

approaching them. "What if someone saw? And besides, it's wasteful."

"Manu lit the lamp at my request, Akori," said the High Priest. "I need it to bless you in the name of the good Gods. Kneel, both of you. Give thanks for the light while you can. There will be darkness aplenty where you are going."

A tight knot of nerves was forming in Akori's stomach. He kneeled.

The High Priest spoke his blessing, his voice grave. Akori kept his eyes on the trembling flame of the oil lamp.

The old priest was right, of course. The darkness of the ordinary world was bad enough, hiding predators and thieves, not to mention hazards like quicksand and deadly snakes and scorpions. But the darkness of the Underworld held dangers a thousand times worse.

"May the light of Ra bless and protect you, for like Ra himself, you must venture into the Underworld..." intoned the priest.

An image leaped into Akori's mind then. On his first quest, he had followed Ra's sun-barge to the entrance of the Underworld. Fortunately, he had freed Ra before the golden barge had vanished into the black opening to begin its night journey.

But the gateway to the Underworld yawned in his mind again now. Akori could still remember the sounds that had come out of it, like vast beasts stirring in nests of human bones. And the stench! Like rotting meat mixed with exotic spices. Manu had said they were funeral balms, used to preserve the bodies of the dead.

He snapped out of the memory. The light burned in his eyes. The High Priest was still speaking.

"...and may they stand strong against all the tricks of the Evil One!" He marked Akori and Manu's foreheads with sacred oil and gestured for them to stand. "You must go," the High Priest said. "Go! Quickly!"

Bidding him farewell, Akori and Manu hurried out into the streets.

Together, Manu and Akori made their way into the city, trying their best to blend in with the bustling crowds. Akori pulled his cloak closer around him, being sure to cover his armour completely. Manu had cleverly put on a shabby old slave's garment and carried a bottle of wine, in the hope people would mistake him for a servant on an errand.

Suddenly, something moved in the corner of Akori's eye. Quickly, he looked around, but there was nothing there but a cat in a doorway, washing itself in an uninterested way.

I'm jumping at shadows, he thought. *Pull yourself together.*

Nobody challenged them as they walked through the city streets and down along the side roads. Traders argued, off-duty soldiers yawned, drinkers in the taverns sang and yelled and called for more wine.

"Not bringing your bags of scrolls this time?" Akori whispered to Manu as they hurried down a street of shops. "What if we need information about the Gods?"

Manu tapped his shiny bald head. "It's all up here now. I've studied a lot. I'm not your High Priest for nothing, Akori."

A flash of dappled fur caught Akori's eye. The cat was there again, trotting along the rooftops, keeping up with them. It was the same cat as before, pale with dark spots.

He was certain of it.

"I think we're being followed," he told Manu with a grin.

"That's what comes of having cats swarming all over your palace!" Manu said. "It wants to be fed, that's all."

Akori thought of shooing it away, but shook his head. So what if one of the palace cats was following him? It wasn't going to tell anyone his real identity, was it?

"This next street's too crowded," he told Manu. "Let's cut down through the back alleys. We can get to the main gate just as easily that way."

The alleys were smellier and a lot darker, but at least there was nobody around to see them. *All we have to do is get out of the city without being seen,* Akori thought. *Once we're outside the walls, this will be easy*.

Then he tripped over something lying in

his path and fell in the dust. A bit of wood? No. It was a leg!

"Hey!" yelled the man who the leg was attached to. His ugly face reared up out of the shadows. "Wash where yer goin', cantcher? Some of us are tryin' to gessum sleep... Hey, wait a minute!"

Akori smelled wine on the man's breath – lots of it. Of all the bad luck!

"So sorry," he said quickly, trying to move past. "Back off to sleep now, goodbye!"

"I said wait!" the man scowled, grabbing Akori's cloak. "I know you, don't I? Seen yer face before, I'm sure of it!"

Akori tried to tug his cloak out of the man's grip while keeping his face turned aside. "Not likely. I'm just a farmer."

The man gave a slow toothless grin.

"I know what it is! You look just like that young Pharaoh, dontcha?"

Manu came to Akori's rescue. "Well he's not!" he said. "And it's a good thing for you that he isn't!"

"Huh?"

Manu folded his arms. "If he was the Pharaoh, he could have you put to death for grabbing him like that."

"Put ter *death*?" the drunkard said fearfully. He let go of Akori's cloak.

"Here," Manu said, passing over the bottle he'd been carrying. "No hard feelings. You can drink to the Pharaoh's health."

The man grabbed the wine greedily. "On yer way," he growled. "You, boy, you should be put ter death for...for...for pretendin' to be the Pharaoh."

Akori and Manu wasted no time getting out of the alley and back onto the main street. "Next time I try to take a shortcut like that," Akori whispered, "kick me, okay?"

"You won't have to ask twice," Manu muttered. Then he frowned. "Although, you do know that's nothing compared to what's waiting for us in the Underworld, don't you?"

"I've heard a few things..." Akori said reluctantly, but Manu was eager to talk.

"The arch-enemy of Ra dwells there. The serpent, Apep! Remember those huge marks we saw on Ra's barge? Apep must have made those."

Akori shuddered to think of a beast large enough to leave scars like that.

"Then there are the demons, and the lakes of fire, and the river of dung," said Manu. "Not to mention the one who swallows up the souls of the unjust dead."

"The Underworld sounds bad enough on a normal day," Akori said, shaking his head. "But with Set in charge, and Osiris imprisoned..."

"Maybe the dead souls down there are the lucky ones." Manu's voice was cold. "After all, they're already dead."

Akori felt a shiver ripple along his spine, thinking of the terrible things that were happening in the Underworld.

It seemed hardly possible. The city was peaceful. All of Egypt was content. From one end of the kingdom to the other, all of Akori's people were safe and well fed.

Could there really be a nightmare realm of ghosts and monsters waiting for them?

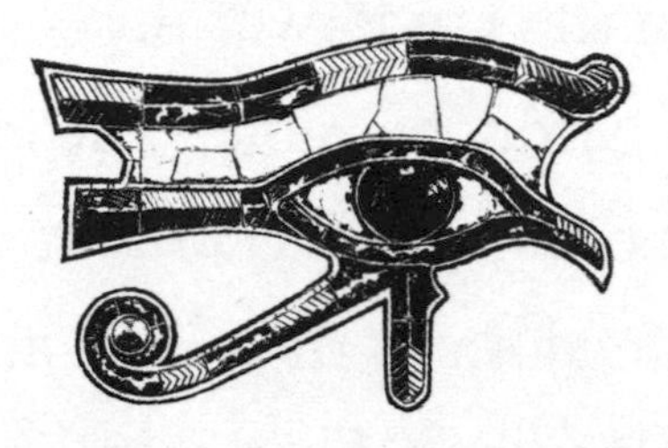

CHAPTER FOUR

A fisherman ferried them across the Nile in his little reed boat, and Akori rewarded him with a nugget of bronze for his trouble. He couldn't help thinking of a very different ferryman that waited in the Underworld. Those *he* took across in his boat never came back.

"There it is!" Manu said. "The Necropolis of Waset!"

An amazing sight now lay before them. Row after row of tombs stretched across the desert sands, some with small mud-brick chapels resting over them. They had marked the resting places of Egyptians and their families for hundreds of years before Akori had even been born.

"I've heard stories of desert ghouls that live among the tombs. They break them open and eat the bones of the dead," Akori said. "They have heads like dogs, and they crunch the bones up. Is that true?"

"I've never seen one," Manu said carefully. "But after what we *have* seen on our travels, I wouldn't be surprised."

Akori slipped his *khopesh* into his hand, and said a silent prayer of thanks to Horus for the golden armour under his cloak.

"We need to go this way," Manu said, leading Akori down a winding path between the tombs. "The royal cemetery is the grandest, most important part of the

Necropolis. The tombs are set into the sides of the hills. Including yours."

"I know. You told me all about it when I became Pharaoh, remember? 'The Valley of the Kings', you called it."

Although Akori hoped it would be many years before he needed to use his tomb, he had still had to have one built during his lifetime so that it was ready in the event of his death, like every other Pharaoh. The entombing of a Pharaoh was too important an event to leave to the last moment. Akori had to view and approve everything, from the carvings and statues to the mummy case.

"We need to hurry," he said. "Sunset can't be far off."

"Can you imagine what it'll be like a thousand years from now?" Manu said proudly, seeming to forget his fear for a moment. "Imagine all the tombs, all the riches! Statues! Jewels! Furniture! There will never be another civilization like ours, Akori. Egypt will last until the end of the world!"

Maybe it will, Akori thought, *but we won't be there to see it. My soul will be with the Gods, but my body will be a shrivelled-up mummy, just like all the mummies in these tombs.*

The thought of visiting his own tomb, his own *coffin,* made his flesh crawl. The riddle Manu had asked him seemed creepy and sinister now. *The man who uses it will have it for ever. We're alone out here except for all the dead,* he thought. *That's not exactly comforting.* To take his mind off it, he looked up at the inscriptions on the tombs as they ran past. Manu had been helping him learn to read over the last few months, and the practice would do him good.

Akori noticed a broad path that branched off to one side, winding down a short distance into the side of a small hill. At the end of the path was a dusty doorway covered in cobwebs but guarded by two statues of ferocious-looking jackals. The whole area was eerily quiet.

"What's down there?" Akori asked, keen to break the silence.

"That's the animal cemetery," Manu explained.

"Really?" said Akori. "But it's so big. The animal in there must have been pretty important."

"Not just one animal," Manu said. "That's a communal tomb. There are dozens of animals in there."

Akori paused, glancing back at the path. He imagined all the different kinds of animals, from the smallest household pets to the Pharaoh's most majestic war horses, mummified and lined up in their own tombs, resting inside. The thought sent an unexpected shudder along his spine.

"Come on, Akori, we need to hurry," said Manu. "If we don't reach your tomb before sunset, we lose our only chance to enter the Underworld."

Akori was just turning away from the cemetery, when there came a sudden, loud scrabbling noise, like a nest of rats fighting violently to get out of a box. Then, just as suddenly, it stopped.

Akori froze, his hand on his sword hilt.

"What was that?" he whispered.

Now came a rasping, grating noise, as if something were scraping long talons against a piece of rough stone. To his horror, Akori realized it was coming from behind the doors of the animal cemetery.

"We should get out of here," Manu said in a fearful voice. "Maybe ghouls are real after all. But I don't want to stay and find out."

A horrendous dry screech echoed up from beneath the earth. Then came a low moan that rose to a rattling cry, as if a dog was howling down a rotten tube of parchment.

"This is very wrong, whatever it is," Akori said. Fighting all his urges to run back the other way, he edged closer to the doors.

"I think something's trapped in there," he whispered. "Maybe a stray dog got in and couldn't get out."

"Maybe," Manu whispered back. He didn't look convinced.

Scrape, scrape, whine, went the thing inside the tomb.

Akori made a decision. "I'm going to break the door down. Get ready."

But before Akori could move, a horrific

wailing, screeching and scratching broke out inside, like the Underworld itself was trying to claw its way through to the surface.

With terrifying certainty, Akori realized that this was no stray dog. It wasn't a living animal at all. It was the sound of hundreds of bone-dry claws angrily raking at the door. Of starving howls ripping through dried-out throats. Of mummy wrappings splitting and cracking, coffins creaking open, clay jars shattering from within. Of a horde of eyeless creatures, brittle and shrunken, mad to tear the flesh of the still-living!

"It's the animal mummies!" Akori yelled. "They're coming back to life. And they're trying to get out!"

Something heavy thumped on the door from inside.

"What did Horus tell us?" said Akori.

"Set is assembling an army of the dead, to wage war on Egypt..."

Thump. A crack appeared across the tomb door. *Thump.*

Manu turned to Akori, horrified. "It is beginning!"

CHAPTER FIVE

The cemetery door cracked again. Next moment it fell crashing to the ground in broken pieces. Framed by the doorway, half-hidden in the shadows and swirling dust, crouched a thing out of Akori's nightmares.

It was, or had once been, a baboon. Now its caved-in, empty-eyed face was almost entirely a skull. The skin had shrivelled back from its teeth in a hideous permanent snarl. Mummy wrappings trailed from its arms.

"Manu, get back!" Akori shouted.

Manu ran back up the path and hid behind a small chapel. Akori braced himself to fight, holding his *khopesh* firmly in a two-handed grip.

The baboon jerked its head up towards the moon. It flung its jaws open, let out a ghastly shriek – and charged. Behind it surged a tide of scuttling, limping, grey-white bodies. Horrified, Akori thought of rats pouring out of a burning barn. There was a host of mummified cats, two more baboons, even something that looked like a mongoose.

They half-ran, half-dragged themselves over the sand, like broken puppets. And was that a *crocodile* mummy behind them all, heaving and flopping out of the tomb?

The lead baboon loped across the sand. Its long arms reached for Akori's neck, to choke the life out of him.

With a wild yell, Akori slashed at it with

his *khopesh.* The razor-sharp metal bit deep.

The baboon's head came flying off its shoulders. The body blundered past, arms still clutching for Akori's throat, and toppled to the ground.

The head rolled over and lay at his feet. The jaws were still opening and closing, trying to bite. Akori staggered backwards with a disgusted cry, and nearly fell over the headless body crawling over the sand looking for him.

Manu grabbed a stone and smashed it down on the baboon's shoulders. The body twitched and lay still.

Akori edged towards a second tomb. *I need to guard my back,* he thought. *These things could come at me from anywhere!*

A chittering, clawed thing came flying at his face. A mummified cat! He sliced it in two with a single blow. The sour dust of the grave burst in clouds around Akori. It burned in his nostrils, choked his throat.

"Akori! Help!" Manu screamed. "They've got me!"

The two other baboon mummies had grabbed Manu and were hauling him out from behind the chapel. Each of them held one of Manu's arms. They were pulling him towards the crocodile mummy! It opened its jaws wide, ready to tear Manu limb from limb.

Akori was still surrounded by swarming cat mummies, clawing at his legs. One of them leaped up onto his body and dangled from his cloak, biting his throat.

With a yell of pain, Akori switched his sword to his right hand and grabbed the cat mummy with his left. It crunched in his grip like a dried-out fruit. The skull squirmed and

yowled, sinking long teeth into the ball of his thumb and drawing fresh blood.

He flung the gruesome thing as hard as he could. It smashed against the tomb wall and fell, limp and broken. It was sickening, but he had no choice. He was fighting for his life.

"Akoriii!" Manu fought to get away from the baboons, but they held him fast. The crocodile mummy was skulking nearer and nearer.

Akori shoved himself away from the tomb wall and ran across the sand. He leaped and brought the *khopesh* down in a scything stroke. The blade sliced a baboon's arm clean off. Manu pulled himself free of the other baboon's grip.

Akori quickly sliced the armless baboon mummy in two at the waist. The other one scampered back away from him.

"Find a weapon!" Akori shouted to Manu.

"There aren't any!"

"Use something! *Anything!*"

Manu grabbed the arm of a broken statue and held it like a club, while Akori faced off against the remaining baboon mummy. It crouched low in the sand and kept its distance. Akori frowned. Was this one cleverer than the others?

Suddenly, the baboon hurled a jagged piece of rock. It slammed into Akori's chest, knocking the wind out of him, flinging him onto his back.

Gasping, he struggled to his feet. Strange – there was no pain at all. The magical armour of Horus must have taken the blow. Without it, Akori's ribs would have shattered like a wooden birdcage.

Akori muttered a curse and dodged out of the way of another flying rock thrown by the baboon mummy. Something clutched at his ankle – the severed baboon arm! He kicked it away. These things just didn't know when they were dead.

The crocodile snapped at Manu. It caught the hem of his cloak in its jaws and tried to drag him off his feet.

Manu staggered. He tried to keep his footing. He fell forwards, but as he did so he brought the stone club down. The crocodile's ancient, brittle skull shattered, caving in like an eggshell.

The baboon leaped up, grabbed the edge of the roof of a chapel and hauled itself up there. It screeched mockingly and began to throw bits of broken masonry.

"I'm going after it!" Akori told Manu. He ducked as a shard of rock whistled over his head. "You should be safe down here. That crocodile was the last of them."

"Okay," Manu said. He held onto the stone arm as if it were the most precious thing in the world. "Good luck."

Akori had to sheathe his *khopesh*. He needed both hands free to climb. Like the baboon had done, he jumped and grabbed the roof, heaving himself up.

The baboon was waiting for him, grinning a lipless grin.

But no sooner had Akori got up there than another beast burst out from a tomb down below. Manu gave a high-pitched scream as the mummified remains of a dog clawed up out of the ground. It shook itself like a wet dog would, but fragments of skin, mummy wrappings and dust flew off it.

The baboon mummy lunged for Akori, huge paws swatting at him. He dodged and weaved, trying desperately to get his sword out.

If any of those blows connected, he'd fall from the roof to the rocky sands below. And while his armour might stop a blow, it couldn't protect him from a fall.

Manu was yelling again. The mummified hound was pacing slowly towards him, growling. Akori knew it could easily tear the young priest's throat out. He had to do something.

The baboon seized Akori round the waist. He felt himself lifted off the ground. It was going to throw him off the roof!

Only one chance. He smashed down with the hilt of his *khopesh* into the thing's face. The paws went slack. Beetles crawled inside the mummy's ruined head.

"Akori!" Manu screamed.

Quickly Akori wrestled himself free, kicked the baboon's body away and looked down over the edge. The dog mummy had backed Manu up against a tomb wall and was snarling at him.

The stone arm trembled in Manu's grip. The dog mummy advanced. There would be blood on the sands any moment now.

Then, to Akori's amazement, the cat that had followed them from the palace came scrambling up onto the roof!

It looked at him with wide, golden eyes.

"Get out of here, cat!" Akori yelled at it. "You won't last a second in this place!"

The cat ignored him. It trotted to the edge of the roof and looked down at Manu, who was cowering as the hound prepared to spring.

The cat jumped. In the instant before it reached the ground, its body stretched, growing huge and long. The beast that landed gracefully on the sand was the size of a lioness.

Akori stared. It couldn't be...

The cat-beast gave a threatening growl. The dog mummy spun around on the spot, just as the huge cat launched itself at it. The gigantic paws knocked it sprawling.

The dog struggled to stand, its legs kicking the sand up.

A single blow, ending in a sharp crack – and it was all over. The mummified dog lay still, never to move again.

Manu ran forwards, crying for joy. "Ebe!"

CHAPTER SIX

One moment the cat-beast was standing before them, casting an enormous shadow across the sand. The next, there was just an ordinary cat again.

She came over to Manu and butted her head against his shin, purring a greeting.

"Ebe?" Manu said. "It *is* you, isn't it?"

The cat hesitated – and nodded.

Akori lowered himself down from the roof and ran over to meet her. "Ebe! You're back!" he laughed. "It's so good to see you again!"

Ebe mewed. She sounded happy.

Akori rubbed her under the chin. "I guess you didn't feel like being a human this time around, huh?"

"She's being smart," Manu said. "Who's going to suspect one little cat of being the Goddess Bast in disguise?"

Akori stroked Ebe's furry back. She arched into his hand happily.

"I don't understand how she can even be here," Akori said. "Didn't Horus say the Gods couldn't help us this time?"

"I thought so...no, wait! Do you remember his exact words? 'Only those who travel with you can help you.'"

"So Ebe's travelling with us?" Akori said delightedly.

Ebe-the-cat nodded again. Then she began to wash her paw in a bored kind of way, as if fighting animal mummies in an ancient cemetery was the most normal thing in the world.

"So we've got a Goddess on our side!" Akori grinned. "That should even the odds a little."

"Not just a Goddess," Manu said. "An old friend."

"Even if she never says a word to us," Akori said with a chuckle. "Some things never change, do they?"

Ebe looked up at him. Her little pink tongue was sticking out.

Akori laughed until his sides hurt.

The three of us are back together again, he thought. *Now I feel like I could take Set on, and all his dark Gods. He couldn't stop us last time, and he won't stop us now.*

"How long until sunset?" he asked Manu.

Manu frowned up at the sky, now awash

with hues of gold and red. "Less than an hour, I'd say. We need to get moving."

"Fine by me. I can't wait to get out of this place."

"You think you can leave my domain so easily?" boomed a mournful voice from beneath the ground. "Little fool. You shall *never* leave!"

Ebe gave a yowl and scooted up to the top of a nearby statue. Her fur stood on end.

A rhythmic crashing sound made the ground shake. Footsteps underground, coming closer – as if something colossal was coming up a set of steps towards them...

"Akori, we should run," said Manu, pulling at his sleeve. "There's no time."

"I'm Pharaoh," Akori said, summoning up his courage. "I don't turn tail and run. Not from anything."

But what he saw then nearly made him eat those bold words.

A terrifying sight came clambering out of a tomb. It was a figure like a man, but over five royal cubits tall, eyes blazing with ghostly fire. Wings like a falcon's spread out from his back and tattered bandages hung from his limbs and body. The sword he carried could have split an ox in two lengthways.

He turned his head to face Akori and breathed out a plume of roaring flames. The tombs flared with hideous light.

"Manu," Akori gulped, "what *is* that?"

"It's Sokar," Manu said. His throat was closing up with sheer fright. "The guardian of tombs! And unless I'm very wrong, he's been bewitched into working for Set!"

Sokar rewarded Manu with a ghoulish leer and a fresh blast of flames. "Protector of the tombs that *you* defiled, little children!" he roared. "Who are you, to break open these sacred resting places and destroy the mummies?"

"We had no choice!" Akori shouted. "We were fighting for our lives!"

"I don't think he's going to listen to reason, Akori!" said Manu.

Sokar bellowed. He struck the ground with his sword.

A zigzag crack opened up in the earth. It grew wider before their eyes. Sand poured in like a waterfall.

Akori looked down into the chasm. To his horror, he saw Sokar's shattering blow had exposed a group of underground tombs. Mummies were stirring down there, clutching up at him with bony arms. If he fell in, they'd tear him to bits!

Sokar leaped over the chasm and stood

ready to fight. Akori quickly looked around. The tomb was to his left, the chasm to his right, and Sokar straight ahead. If he turned around, he might be able to run back to the path...

He shook his head. There was no running away from this fight. "Come on!" he yelled instead. "If you're going to fight me, then fight me!"

Sokar laughed, as if to mock Akori's bravery. He swung his great sword at him, perhaps thinking this would all be over in seconds.

Akori blocked it. Metal screeched and sparks flew.

Sokar blinked. "You dare..."

He never finished the sentence. Akori launched into a furious attack.

He rained down blows with his *khopesh* so hard and fast it was like a shimmer of gold around him. Sokar barely brought his own sword up in time to parry.

The bewildered dark God found he was falling back before the onslaught. Akori slashed and struck, spinning around on the spot for extra force.

"Come on, Akori!" Manu cheered. "Send him back to the Underworld!"

Deep, bloodless gashes began to appear on Sokar's body where the blade had hit home. The mummy wrappings that covered him were dangling loose now. And still Akori came, like a hurricane of gold, brown and white.

Sokar took another step back as Akori made yet another fierce cut. Now, Sokar was standing on the very edge of the chasm he himself had opened up. The low moaning of a hundred mummies came from the smashed-open tombs below.

One good hard blow should knock Sokar off his feet and send him tumbling into the chasm. Akori raised his *khopesh*, ready to finish this.

Sokar lashed out with sudden, blinding speed. His sword struck Akori's and knocked it flying out of his grasp.

It landed on the other side of the chasm, far beyond reach.

Akori stood dumbfounded. He had no weapon...

An evil, hungry sneer began to spread across Sokar's face. Slowly, maliciously, he raised his sword.

"What will you do now, *little boy*?" Sokar thundered.

Chapter Seven

Fear ran icy steel needles through Akori's stomach. Never before had he faced such an opponent without even having a weapon in his hand.

This was impossible. He *couldn't* win. Sokar would surely kill him. The quest was over before it had begun – unless he turned and ran, ran for his life without looking back.

He glanced over his shoulder. Manu and Ebe were behind him, both wide-eyed and frightened out of their wits. They had good reason to be. Once Sokar had finished with him, they would be next.

Then he saw a familiar piece of stone lying on the sand – the statue's arm that Manu had used as a club – and he knew what he had to do. He grabbed it and stood ready to fight again.

"I am no 'little boy'," he shouted bravely up at Sokar. "I am Pharaoh of all Egypt, ally of the good Gods, and the champion of Horus. If you think you can defeat me, then *go ahead and try*!"

Just for a second, uncertainty showed on Sokar's arrogant face.

Then, with a snarl, he smashed his sword down where Akori stood.

Akori dived out of the way just in time and gave Sokar's arm a powerful whack with his stone club.

The God moaned in surprise and pain. He dealt out two-handed blows to this side and that, pounding the earth with his sword like a blacksmith bashing the dents out of a piece of metal. But no matter how hard he tried to slice Akori in two, Akori was quicker on his feet and always ducked away at the last moment.

I have to even the odds, Akori thought desperately, as he dodged yet another ringing blow. *I can't keep jumping about like a gazelle for ever – he'll tire me out!*

Then he saw his bravery was catching. Manu, determined to help, had circled around to Sokar's side and was tugging at his bandages! The God was ignoring Manu completely, as if he wasn't even worth his attention. His gaze was fixed on Akori as he readied another blow.

Sokar's huge sword crashed into the

ground near Akori, spattering him with sand and churned earth. That was too close!

Akori was panting heavily now, worn out by the effort of dodging Sokar's blows. Sokar, on the other hand, wasn't flagging at all. The God was just too strong! That sword of his could split solid stone!

An idea came into Akori's mind. He glanced around, and found what he was looking for almost instantly – a thick stone slab a short distance behind him, fallen from a forgotten tomb.

Now he just had to time his leaps perfectly, so Sokar wouldn't suspect anything.

He sidestepped Sokar's next blow, then stepped cautiously backwards, hoping Sokar would think he was losing the will to fight.

The God took the bait and stepped forwards, grinning. Manu was still tugging at

Sokar's loose bandages, gradually unravelling them, exposing his putrid flesh.

Sokar struck out again. Akori jumped backwards. Again – and now Akori was standing on the stone slab.

This would be the hardest part of all. He'd have to pretend he'd given up.

He stood still, his club by his side, and waited for Sokar's final blow.

"You face your death bravely," Sokar hissed, readying his sword. "I admit, you have been a worthy foe. But you will be just as dead for all that!"

Akori said nothing. He set his jaw and glared defiantly into Sokar's hideous face.

Sokar swung his sword with all his might.

At the crucial last moment, Akori dodged. Sokar's blade sliced deep into the stone. Akori could only hope it was deep enough...

"So, a coward after all," Sokar sneered.

He tugged at his sword, trying to pull it free from the stone, but it was stuck fast.

"No!" he bellowed. "Wretch! You dare deceive *me*?"

Now, Akori thought, *while he's good and angry*.

Akori ran back to the edge of the chasm. Sokar abandoned his trapped sword and came lumbering after him, a maddened giant.

Manu caught Akori's eye and gave him a quick nod to say he was ready. As Sokar came charging past, Manu grabbed the end of a loose bandage and ran around the base of a statue, pulling it taut.

Now he just needed Ebe to do her part. There she was, in giant cat form once again, bounding silently behind Sokar.

As the God roared and charged, Ebe launched herself through the air and knocked the God off his feet. Manu hauled on Sokar's bandage at the same time.

The God stumbled, staggered, and with a dreadful yell went tumbling into the open chasm. Hundreds of mummified arms clutched at him as he fell. A violent crash shook the earth as he hit the bottom.

"He's down!" Akori shouted. "Now we just have to make sure he stays that way!"

They looked down. Sokar lay groaning, far beneath them. He was stunned now, but soon he'd recover. Then he would be on their heels again.

"Sokar's magic opened up that chasm," Manu said. "Maybe one God can break the magic of another. Or...a Goddess?"

Ebe nodded her tawny head. She laid a paw on the edge of the pit and her eyes blazed with a fierce golden light. A deep grinding rumble sounded and the chasm closed, trapping the groaning Sokar in its depths like a mummy in a walled-up tomb.

Akori glanced quickly at the horizon. The fight had taken up valuable time. Already the sky was darkening and night was creeping ever closer. They had to reach the Valley of the Kings before sunset, or else they would fail in their quest to save Egypt.

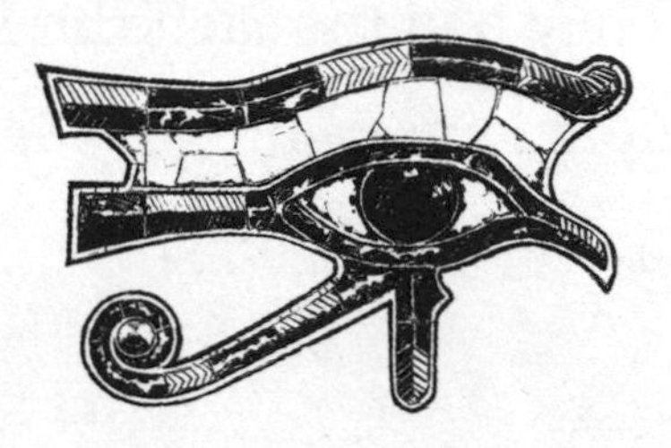

CHAPTER EIGHT

"No time to celebrate," Akori warned them. "All this was for nothing unless we can make it to my tomb before the sun comes up."

Akori quickly retrieved his *khopesh* before Manu led them back to the path and pointed up to the hills ahead. "We should make it, but we'll have to hurry."

"Shame Ebe can't carry us!" Akori said.

"She has to conserve her power. A God in mortal form is limited in what they can do," Manu reminded him.

Ebe, shrunk to small size again, went racing ahead of them with her tail held high. As Akori set off after her, a deep groan resounded from below the earth. Sokar was clearly angry, and trying to dig his way out! Akori put on a fresh burst of speed.

The three of them ran as fast as they could. They passed sprawling tomb complexes where families had lain interred for hundreds of years and humble graves that were nothing more than a mound of dirt with a wooden marker.

Again and again, Akori looked back over his shoulder at the western horizon, certain that he would soon see the sun disappear completely, spelling total disaster. They had to get to the tomb before nightfall, Horus had said.

Eventually, winded and footsore, they reached the rocky slope-sided region that

Manu had called the Valley of the Kings. Dark cave mouths gaped up on the hillsides, the entrances to royal tombs from before Akori's time.

"They're...high up...to discourage tomb robbers," Manu panted, answering a question that nobody had asked.

There was nothing for it but to climb – a wearying, punishing climb that left Akori's limbs aching. Even the sight of his own tomb's entrance, when at last it came into view beyond a bulge of rock, hardly troubled him now. He was so worn out, he wondered if he would fall asleep in his own coffin.

It was strange to think that when he'd woken up this morning, it had seemed like an ordinary day – as ordinary as being Pharaoh would ever be, that is. Now here he was, about to enter the Underworld.

Ebe wasn't bothered by the climb at all. She hopped from rock to rock, looked back at them anxiously and climbed further. Akori remembered how easily she'd climbed up the sheer rock face on their very first quest. They should have guessed there was something of the cat about her a lot sooner...

"Hurry!" Manu yelled from behind him. "We need to get inside!"

Akori scrambled up the last ledge and walked warily into the open tomb. Ebe came with him, swishing her tail impatiently Lights were glimmering from inside. He froze. Facing him from the other end of the hallway was – his own face! It was a carved stone bust of him wearing the Double Crown. Its blank, empty eyes stared at him like a foretaste of his own death. *At least I have the right tomb,* he thought.

"Akori!" came the panicked cry from outside. "The sun's setting!"

Akori didn't want to go anywhere near that creepy stone face, but he took a deep breath and pushed past it into the main burial chamber.

Light came from flickering oil lamps on little ledges in the wall. Akori's sarcophagus awaited him. Mysterious-looking hieroglyphs covered its sides. On the top was an image of Akori himself; he shuddered at the sight of it. Akori tried to shove the lid off. Manu came to help him, and between them they shifted the massive slab enough to expose what lay within.

Inside the stone sarcophagus was a second coffin, this one a mummy case made from wood. It gleamed with gold leaf and bright blue lapis lazuli.

Akori was relieved to see the face wasn't

a very good likeness this time, but it still gave him the creeps to see it. Climbing into your own coffin seemed too much like inviting death to come and claim you. Outside it was growing ever darker. The sun was sinking below the horizon...

Akori heaved the coffin open. "Everyone get inside," he said. "It's going to be cramped, but it's what Horus said to do."

He clambered unsteadily into the open mummy case. Manu followed, pressed up against him, breathing heavily. His flesh felt clammy and cold against Akori's skin. Akori realized he must be terrified. Ebe nestled at their feet, a comforting warm presence. He lowered the lid of the coffin on top of them. They lay together in darkness for a few moments. There was no sound but their breathing.

"Now what?" whispered Manu.

"I don't know," Akori whispered back. "I guess we just wait."

But no sooner had he said that than a dim blue light began to appear. Glowing hieroglyphs were appearing on the inside of the casket lid, as if an invisible stylus was scratching the darkness away.

"Can you read that?" Manu asked, awed. "It's a bit beyond what we've been practising with."

Manu was right. This was way beyond *Ankhesenamun likes the dog* and *See Tuthmose run.* But Akori was determined to try. His lips moved as he read the symbols.

"It's a coffin text!" he burst out. "You told me about these!"

"That's right," Manu said. "A magical verse, to help the dead Pharaoh's soul make it through the challenges of the Underworld. They're meant for dead people to read, but this one looks like it's meant for us."

Akori hesitated. "Should I read it out? It... won't pull my soul out of my body, will it?"

"We'll read it together," Manu said firmly. "That way, whatever happens will happen to us both."

"Ready?"

"Let's do this."

Together, they began to read the ominous-looking text. Even in that tiny, cramped space, the words seemed to echo. From somewhere, a whispering inhuman voice was reading the words along with them:

"I shall sail rightly in my vessel, I am Lord of Eternity in the crossing of the sky..."

As they read the coffin text, the writing blazed brighter, the unseen stylus wrote faster and faster, and the whole coffin suddenly began to tremble...

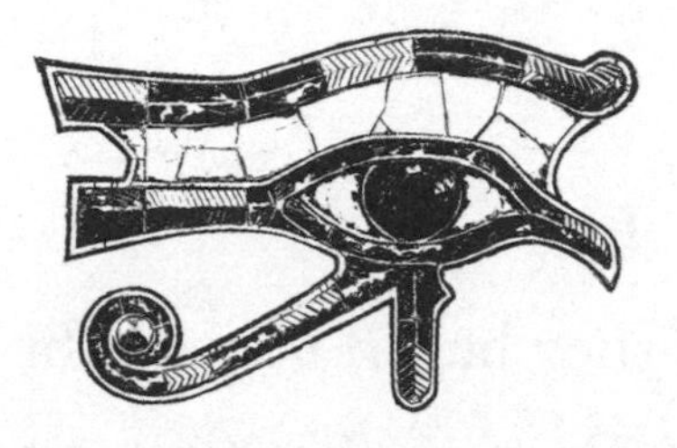

CHAPTER NINE

Akori badly wanted to ask Manu if he knew what was going on, but he didn't dare stop chanting. They were halfway through the coffin text, and the more they read, the more the coffin shook and shuddered around them.

Bump, rattle, bump. It felt as if the flimsy wooden coffin was sliding down the side of a rocky mountain, about to fly off into space. The very next second, Akori's heart lurched as a rushing sensation took over from the bumps and rattles. *Maybe we have flown off the edge of a cliff,* he thought. His mouth was dry with fear, but he forced himself to keep chanting. Beside him, Manu nervously accompanied him. Was that whistling wind he could hear? The coffin was definitely falling through space now. Akori felt weightless – that horrid feeling of having missed a step, just before you jar your leg.

His mind raced with images as he tried to imagine what was happening to them. Maybe a hidden panel had opened in the tomb, sending the coffin and its three frightened occupants hurtling down a rocky chute before ejecting them in some unknown underground cavern. Or maybe – it almost stopped Akori's heart with fear to think about it – Sokar had found them, picked the coffin up, shaken it furiously and hurled it high into the sky.

Whatever was happening to them, one thing was for sure. It couldn't go on for ever. Any fall, no matter how unexpected, always had to end in a landing. And it seemed horribly likely that this would be a crash landing.

They were coming to the very end of the coffin text. Akori knew, by some deep instinct, that it would also mark the end of their strange journey. He braced himself for the impact.

They read the last syllable. Akori closed his eyes. Soon there would be splintering wood, screams and agony.

But the crash never came.

There was a new sound, a rhythmic, splashing noise. It sounded like someone washing clothes on the bank of the Nile, or like something dipping into the water and coming out again.

Akori had to see where they were. Very cautiously, he lifted the lid of the coffin. What he saw nearly made him drop the lid in fright. The tomb walls that had surrounded them had vanished. They were on board a boat. Only a flaming torch at the bow gave any light. They were being rowed through darkness.

This must be the land of the dead, he thought. *Everything I've ever known – fields, houses, the palace – is now far beyond our reach. This is it. We're in the Underworld.*

The splashing sound was coming from two long jet-black oars that propelled the boat along. The man holding the oars was tall and muscular. But although his body faced the coffin, his head was twisted completely in the opposite direction.

"We're on Aken's barge," Akori told the others breathlessly. Ebe mewed her assent.

Akori had encountered Aken before. He was the ferryman of Anubis, who took the souls of the dead down into the Underworld. He couldn't be reasoned with, and no threat would make him turn his boat around. He only ever made one journey – and those he brought with him, as Akori knew all too well, never returned.

Akori had tricked him once. He'd used the Talisman of Ra to make Aken think it was still daylight, cleverly keeping the barge from descending into the Underworld and taking Manu, Akori and Ebe down with it.

"Pray he doesn't recognize you," Manu said. "He might not be happy about the way we deceived him before…"

But Aken didn't turn around. He didn't even act like he remembered Akori from before. He just kept rowing and rowing, as if he was in a trance.

"There's no going back now," Akori whispered. "Aken's barge has sunk down into the Underworld and taken us with it."

Aken was rowing his barge down a bubbling black river. It was the same size and shape as the Nile, but seemed to be made of liquid darkness. The burning torch cast no reflection in its troubled surface. Akori could only just make out the riverbank, far in the distance.

"Horus said we have to follow the path taken by the dead," said Manu. "The first caverns of the Underworld are horrible enough at the best of times. But with Set in charge? It's going to be like a nightmare come true."

Akori clenched his jaw and tried not to think about it.

"I've read about the worst parts of the Underworld in the scrolls," Manu kept on.

"Monstrous beasts, waiting to tear you to pieces and devour you. Lakes of scorching fire; terrible tortures too terrifying to imagine."

Akori tensed all over, unable to drive the horrible images from his mind. "Please shut up!" he groaned.

"And you know what's waiting at the end of it all, don't you?" Manu said, ignoring Akori's pleas. "Ammit, the Eater of Souls. A horrendous hybrid monster that can devour the soul of any being in creation. I expect even a God would never come back if Ammit swallowed them up—"

Ebe hissed furiously. *She doesn't want to listen to him any more than I do,* Akori thought.

Finally the message seemed to sink in. Manu fell silent. He didn't speak again for a long time.

Akori suddenly noticed the riverbank was much closer now. "Follow me," he said, cautiously leading Manu and Ebe out of the coffin.

"Do we swim?" Manu said fearfully.

Ebe gave a yowl of protest at the idea.

Akori looked at the bank. "I don't think we'll have to," he said excitedly. "Aken's coming close to the land. When we get near enough, we'll jump."

Aken showed no sign of having heard them. Still, Akori didn't want to alert him to their escape. They were his cargo, after all, and he might not appreciate it...

"Ready?" Akori said as the bank drew closer. "Now!"

One after the other, they leaped onto the shore.

Off in the distance, Akori could just make out the shape of a gigantic archway closed off by an enormous gate.

"That must be the Gate we need to open," he said. "Manu? What do you think?"

"I don't know, Akori," Manu said, sounding completely lost. "Everything seems completely different from the ancient guides."

"Maybe Set's made some changes since he's been in charge," Akori said grimly. "The Underworld is supposed to be a place where the dead are judged fairly, right? I can see why Set would want to change that."

"Oh, I think there have been some changes all right," Manu stammered. "Akori, look..."

Lumbering towards them was a terrifyingly familiar sight. The gigantic figure of Sokar, his mouth flaming, was charging at them.

Even worse was the monster that followed behind Sokar, beside which he looked like a small child. It was a scaled, hideous creature as large as a house, with the body of a crocodile and the head of a hippopotamus. The mouth gaped wide, wide enough to swallow all three of them whole...

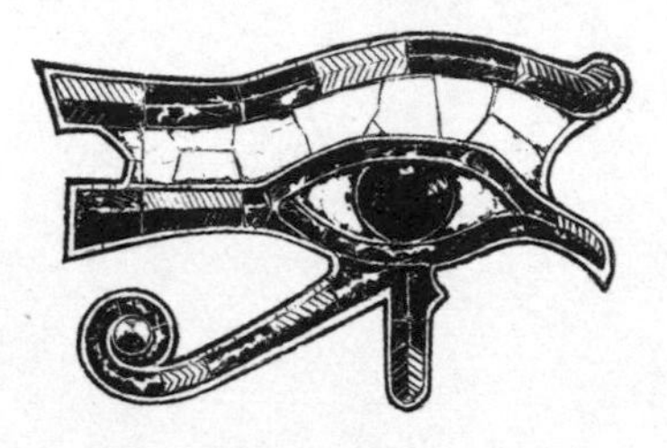

Chapter Ten

"Trespassers!" Sokar roared. "You have entered the domain of Set!"

"The domain of Osiris!" Akori yelled back defiantly.

Sokar gave a sinister laugh and stood with his arms folded. "Not any longer. The old order has been destroyed. My master and his champion are Lords of the Underworld now."

"I gave his so-called champion something to remember me by, last time we met," snarled Akori, brandishing his *khopesh* dangerously. "Does it still sting?"

Sokar snorted in contempt. "Enough of this foolishness. There is a sacrifice to be made." He beckoned, and the immense monster behind him came thundering forwards.

"What is that thing?" Akori whispered to Manu.

"Its name is secret," Manu said. He was shaking so hard he could hardly get the words out. "It's the Guardian of the Gate."

"So what did he mean by a sacrifice?"

With astounding speed for something so huge, the Guardian lunged its open mouth at Ebe.

"No!" Akori yelled and flung himself at her.

He snatched up the terrified cat just in time. The huge mouth slammed shut only a hair's breadth away from him. A stench of putrid meat came from the huge flared nostrils, making Akori feel sick.

"Back!" Sokar barked at it.

The Guardian slowly sat back on its haunches. It stared greedily at Ebe, who nestled in Akori's arms, shivering.

Sokar patted its huge flank. "Patience. Soon you shall feast." He turned to Akori. "My master could destroy you all in an instant, but it amuses him to present you with a choice instead."

"Choice?" Akori asked. Why wasn't Sokar attacking?

"This is the Gate to the deeper levels of the Underworld," Sokar declared. "Only one thing can open it. The Guardian must be fed a sacrifice. And only a living being will satisfy her terrible hunger. Obviously, you cannot be devoured, since you wish to confront Set. So you must choose. Which of your companions will you feed to the Guardian? The cat...or the priest?"

"What makes you think I'd betray my friends?" Akori shouted.

"You have no choice," Sokar leered. "The most powerful spells of Thoth's book are holding that Gate shut. Wait a million years, send a million armies to batter it down – nothing will work! But a single living soul, swallowed up by the Guardian, will open the Gate for ever."

Manu and Ebe both stared at Akori. Neither of them could move. Sheer terror seemed to hold them both in a freezing grip. To die was one thing, but to have your immortal soul devoured by this beast? It was unthinkable...

"Choose now, Pharaoh!" roared Sokar. "Send one of them to be devoured, or the Guardian will choose for you. And I think she prefers the little cat."

The Guardian of the Gate slowly opened its colossal mouth and leaned forwards.

Ebe trembled. The hot oven of the Guardian's throat yawned before Akori.

"I have chosen," he said.

He held Ebe in both his hands and threw her as hard as he could – *away* from the Guardian's gaping mouth.

Fear threatened to freeze him in his tracks. He had to act now, before the mouth closed. If he didn't move now he never would.

Akori drew his *khopesh* and ran towards the Guardian. He leaped into her wide open mouth, flew between her jaws and landed on the swampy surface of her tongue. The whole mouth tilted as the startled Guardian, in a reflex action, swallowed him whole. The last thing Akori heard was Sokar's cry of surprise. Then he was sliding through stinking darkness, tumbling head over heels into a squelching morass of unspeakable horror inside the Guardian's stomach.

He was trapped in a stifling, slime-coated pocket of hot flesh. The smell was indescribable. Juices stung his arms and legs, burning like flaming oil. Pulsing wet surfaces surrounded him on all sides, pressing in so hard he could hardly move. *Horus, be with me now,* he silently prayed.

He slashed at the Guardian with the *khopesh.* She roared in agony, shaking Akori around in the sloshing loathsomeness of her gullet. Akori hacked again and again, ripping through the monster, laying bare ribs as huge as trees. It was ghastly work. Akori could hardly breathe. Filth slimed him from head to toe. Every sword stroke made the Guardian bellow, jostling Akori around so he couldn't tell which way was up or down. Then, right when he least expected it, he saw a light shining. Something like a hot coal was glimmering faintly through the sludge in the Guardian's bowels.

It's one of the Pharaoh Stones! He grabbed it. A thrill of power surged through his fingers, flooding up his arm and across his chest. His heart felt as if it was encircled by bands of living fire.

He pressed it into place in the socket in his armour. Fresh courage filled him. Emboldened, he swung and hacked, scything the monster's flesh off in great rippling sheets like a ship's sails. With a valiant final slash, he tore a long rip in the Guardian's side. Light blazed in.

Breathing hard, Akori clambered out of the monster's belly.

Outside, Ebe was in her cat-beast form, fighting Sokar with fangs and claws, while Manu darted around trying helplessly to do some good. Sokar was laughing at them both, as if they presented no threat at all, and he was just passing the time. But when Akori stood up in front of him, with the Stone blazing in his breastplate, Sokar stood dumbfounded. His sword hung limp at his side and his mouth gaped open.

"Your Guardian has been gutted," snarled Akori. "Do you want to be next?"

All Sokar's rage had gone and now only fear was left. "The Stone of Courage! You... did...how...?"

Akori levelled his *khopesh* at him. "The Gate. Open it. Now."

"It opened when the Guardian swallowed you!" Sokar said. "But you...you..."

"I never promised to *stay* swallowed," Akori said with a fierce grin of victory. " As for you, Sokar? Maybe I'll let you live. You can take a message for me. Run back to your master."

"What...should I tell him, mighty Pharaoh?" Sokar grovelled.

"Nothing," Akori said.

"I don't understand."

"Tell him nothing. Just let him see the fear on your face."

Sokar stared. He looked at Akori's steady eyes, the dripping sword in his hand and the mighty Guardian slain.

Then without another word he turned and ran, his huge feet slamming on the sand, and vanished through the distant Gate.

Chapter Eleven

"Come on," Akori urged. "We need to get back to the palace."

"Um, just one question, Akori," said Manu. "*How* do we get back to the upper world?"

Akori's moment of victory vanished in a cold wind of fresh fear. He'd been so determined to reach the Gate that he'd not given a single thought to the return journey. Too late, Horus's warning came back into his mind: *After each battle, you must make it back out of the Underworld by sunrise.*

If you do not, then the Underworld will claim you for ever.

"I don't know," he said. "But we've got until sunrise to do it – hey, Ebe, wait! Where are you going? Ebe!"

The cat was racing back the way they had come, over the scarlet sands and towards the black river. Akori and Manu traded glances and ran after her. If anyone knew the way out of the Underworld, Akori thought, it would be the Cat Goddess.

They reached the bank of the river just in time to see Aken's barge heading into a pitch-black tunnel mouth in the wall of the cavern. With Ebe in the lead they raced along the bank, trying desperately to reach the barge before it disappeared from sight. Aken was rowing very slowly, still locked in the trance of his endless task. He didn't look around at the approaching trio. The barge was more than halfway into the tunnel now.

"Jump!" Akori shouted.

Ebe sprang and landed safely on the barge. Akori jumped after her and landed hard, scraping his shin.

Manu jumped and fell with a splash into the black river. He clung to the side of the barge, yelling in panic. Quickly Akori helped him up, just as an ominous ripple began to move through the water towards him. The barge glided into the echoing rock tunnel. Manu shivered.

"Thanks. That was too close – hey, look at the Stone glowing on your chest!" A ruby-red light was shining through the filthy cloth of Akori's cloak. He opened it and admired the splendour of the fiery jewel set into his golden armour.

"How does it feel?" Manu asked him, in tones of awe.

"It's incredible," Akori told him. "I can feel the power running through me. It's like fire in my blood."

"We're one step closer to defeating Oba and Set!" Manu smiled.

Ebe scratched at the coffin with her claws and mewed.

Akori understood. "We need to get back inside," he said. "That's how we got in, so I guess it's how we get out."

"I hope so," Manu said, climbing in. "Because if it's not, we'll be stuck in here for a long time!"

Once they were all inside, Akori closed the lid. The glow from the Stone of Courage lit up the inside of the coffin with an eerie red glare. *It's like my heart is burning*, Akori thought proudly.

Just like before, the coffin shuddered and there was a sense of falling through endless space. Then everything went quiet. Akori listened for the splash of Aken's oars on the water, but heard nothing at all. Cautiously he lifted the coffin lid.

"We're back in my tomb in the Valley of the Kings!" he said, feeling immense relief. "I never thought I'd be so glad to see my own tomb."

After the horrors of the Underworld, the short journey back to the palace was like paradise. The clean, fresh air had never smelled so good. Akori noticed the people seemed more troubled than they had before, though. An anxious mood seemed to hang over the city.

They had to sneak back in through the unguarded rear entrance. Akori found the High Priest pacing up and down in his chambers. His face broke into a smile as soon as he heard Akori's voice.

"We made it!" Akori said. "And I've claimed the first of the Pharaoh Stones!"

"Wonderful!" the High Priest said. "And it is good to have Ebe back with us, whatever form she chooses to wear!"

Akori excitedly told the story of the last twenty-four hours, from the battle in the animal cemetery to his courageous jump into the Guardian's gaping mouth. The High Priest listened, nodding solemnly.

"I can see why the Stone of Courage was gifted to you," he commented. "To leap willingly into the mouth of such a monster, without knowing if you could possibly survive...that is the bravest deed I have ever heard of."

"Thank you," Akori said modestly.

"You must rest while you can, for Horus will surely call upon you again soon," the High Priest said. "I have listened to the gossip of the guardsmen and the reports from the high officials, and they all agree one thing. Rumours are spreading across Egypt, rumours of strange noises coming from tombs, of mummies walking by night. The Enemy is making ready to invade us."

The Stone tingled Akori's fingers as he touched it again. Now he had its power to draw upon, the challenges to come might not be as impossible as he'd feared.

He smiled. "I'm ready."

EPILOGUE

"He gave you no message at all?" Oba demanded.

"None," said Sokar. He was on his knees beside the lake of fire, hanging his head in shame.

Oba stood with his hands on his hips. Behind him loomed Set, silent as a carven statue.

"So the Guardian of the Gate is slain, cut open from the inside," Oba said slowly. "Because the boy chose to throw himself into the Guardian's mouth as a sacrifice?"

"It wasn't supposed to happen that way," moaned Sokar. "He was supposed to choose which of his companions to sacrifice. We never thought he would choose himself*!"*

"YOU never thought," Oba corrected him. Then his eyes narrowed. "Lift your head. Look at me."

"My Lord, I beg you, no..."

"Look at me!"

Oba stared long and hard at Sokar's face. He thought for a moment that Sokar was terrified of him, but slowly he realized the God was much more afraid of Akori. Anger swept over him in a hot wave.

"Set!" Oba screeched. "Let this incompetent fool wash off the stink of his failure in the lake of fire!"

Sokar screamed and begged for mercy, but Oba was deaf to his pleas. Set grabbed him, hoisted him up and threw him far into the centre of the flaming lake. A jet of flames shot up as the flailing God went under...and the screaming ceased.

"Burn!" Oba yelled after him. "Ten

thousand years of roasting to a cinder will teach you what it means to fail me."

"A fitting punishment," Set mused. "It will serve as a warning to the others."

Oba stood glaring at the flames, his teeth still bared in anger. Then his mouth twisted into a sly smile.

"Come, my old friend," he said to Set. "Our enemy will soon be returning to the Underworld. And I am going to make sure he never gets out again."

COLLECT EVERY QUEST

ATTACK OF THE SCORPION RIDERS

For his first quest, Akori must risk his life, fighting giant scorpions and a hideous Snake Goddess. Will he be victorious?

ISBN 9781409521051

CURSE OF THE DEMON DOG

The dead are stalking the living and it's up to Akori to stop them – but a scary dog-headed hunter is on his trail!

ISBN 9781409521068

BATTLE OF THE CROCODILE KING

Akori must brave the Nile to battle two evil Gods – the terrifying Crocodile King, and the bloodthirsty Frog Goddess.

ISBN 9781409521075

LAIR OF THE WINGED MONSTER

Vicious vultures and deadly beasts lie in wait for Akori as he searches the desert for the Hidden Fortress of Fire.

ISBN 9781409521082

SHADOW OF THE STORM LORD

Akori must fight Set, the dark Lord of Storms himself, and beat the evil Pharaoh Oba, in his deadliest battle yet.

ISBN 9781409521099

FREE GAME CARDS IN EVERY BOOK!

FIGHT OF THE FALCON GOD

Young Pharaoh Akori ventures into the Underworld to battle the fearsome Falcon God. But can he make it out alive?

ISBN 9781409562009

RISE OF THE HORNED WARRIOR

Akori must escape from the Underworld labyrinth of bones and overcome the lightning-fast Lord of Thunder.

ISBN 9781409562023

SCREAM OF THE BABOON KING

Akori journeys to Oba's Underworld palace, where he confronts his nightmares in the form of the evil Baboon God.

ISBN 9781409562047

CLASH OF THE DARK SERPENT

The Sun God has been captured by the gigantic serpent of the Underworld. Will Akori be able to defeat the awesome beast?

ISBN 9781409562061

DESCENT OF THE SOUL DESTROYER

Akori faces the ultimate challenge when he reaches the heart of the Underworld and meets the monstrous Soul Devourer.

ISBN 9781409562085

THERE'S A WHOLE WORLD OF GODS AND MONSTERS WAITING TO BE EXPLORED AT...

Check out all the game cards online and work out which ones YOU'LL need to beat your friends

Discover exclusive new games to play with your collectable cards

Investigate an interactive map of ancient Egypt

Get tips on how to write top-secret messages in hieroglyphics

Find out the goriest facts and grossest info on ancient Egypt

Download cool guides to the gods, amazing Egyptian make-and-do activities, plus loads more!

LOG ON NOW!

WWW.QUESTOFTHEGODS.CO.UK